TALE from the LABYRINTH

LEGENDS FROM
KING ARTHUR'S LABYRINTH
REIMAGINED BY

JAYNE DOCKSEY

Cover Illustration by Fotokostic
Tale Illustrations by Kevin McTomney
Book design by Ian Clewett | Formation Creative

Published by Corris Caverns Ltd. Machynlleth SY20 9RF
Printed by Book Printing UK www.bookprintinguk.com
Remus House, Coltsfoot Drive, Peterborough, PE2 9BF

Printed in Great Britain
Although every precaution has been taken in the preparation of this book,
the publisher and author assume no responsibility for errors or omissions.
Neither is any liability assumed for damages resulting from the use of
information contained herein.

ISBN 978-0-9954992-0-1

TALES

IN THE BEGINNING...

UNDER THE MOUNTAINS OF SOUTHERN SNOWDONIA
NEAR THE PICTURESQUE VILLAGE OF CORRIS LIES A
MAZE OF WINDING TUNNELS AND ENORMOUS CAVERNS.

HERE, DEEP UNDERGROUND IN KING ARTHUR'S LABYRINTH,
CERYS, A YOUNG GIRL, FALLS INTO A TRANCE IN WHICH
SHE MEETS AN ANCIENT BARD. HE TRANSPORTS HER BACK
BY BOAT INTO THE DARK AGES; A TIME OF MYTH, MAGIC,
DRAGONS AND GIANTS WHEN THE STORIES OF KING ARTHUR
WERE FIRST TOLD.

THE TALES ARE SET ONE THOUSAND FIVE HUNDRED
YEARS AGO WHEN THE ROMAN LEGIONS HAD DEPARTED
FROM BRITAIN LEAVING THE BRITONS TO DEFEND THEMSELVES
AGAINST THE INVADING SAXONS. THE ANCIENT WELSH
LEGENDS OF THIS TIME HAVE BEEN HANDED DOWN OVER
THE CENTURIES BY BARDS, POETS AND STORYTELLERS.
THEY COME TO LIFE AS CERYS AND HER COMPANION TRAVEL
BACK IN TIME THROUGH THE LABYRINTH.

THE LEGENDS HEARD BY CERYS UNFOLD IN THE
FOLLOWING PAGES.

MYRDDIN AND THE TWO DRAGONS

Myrddin glanced over his shoulder as he careered his way through an uneven carpet of twigs and crunchy leaves. The yellow daffodils he had been picking when he first heard Dinabutius's shouts were gripped in his hand.

The forest had suddenly become a frightening place. A dark cloud smothered the sun and the green leaves began a swirling waltz around the ash trees.

Dinabutius had been his enemy since he discovered that Myrddin did not have a father. He was fourteen, a year older than Myrddin, and considered himself better than everyone else because of his royal heritage. His tongue always poked through his lips giving him the appearance of not being very bright.

Myrddin was not scared of him but wise enough to know that if he fought a boy with royal blood there would be severe consequences. The last time he had punched Dinabutius and splattered his nose, he was put into the stocks and pelted with mouldy fruit. He was too proud to go through that humiliation again and decided that hiding in the undergrowth would be the cleverest option.

Leaping through the brambles, Myrddin was making good progress when a fiendish vine snaked its way tightly around his ankle and brought him sprawling to the ground. Taking a small knife from his belt he started to hack himself free.

Suddenly his hands froze. Somebody was breathing close behind him. Slowly, he inched his neck around.

Dinabutius towered above him. His tongue poked through his bloodless lips and the mean smile he wore transformed his handsome features.

"Well, boy without a father," he hissed. "Did I not warn you what would happen if you came into my woods again?"

Pulling his grey tunic over his knees Myrddin looked at the broken daffodils beside him.

Dinabutius followed his gaze.

"Flowers, Myrddin?" The buttons on his red silk tunic strained as he swooped down to pick up the bunch. "Have you found yourself a girlfriend?"

"They're for my mother" muttered Myrddin, going bright red.

Dinabutius brought the daffodils to his nose with an exaggerated sniff.

"How sweet" he said.

Myrddin's blood began to boil. He hated Dinabutius so much.

"How can you expect somebody of my status to treat a peasant any differently, Myrddin? You are not my equal. My parents are both of royal blood. I know who I am and where I'm from. You are a nobody without a true identity. No one knows who your father is – although word has it that he's the Devil."

Myrddin sprang to his feet shaking from head to foot with rage. He bent his head and hurled himself at Dinabutius's belly.

The boys wrestled in the mud. Twigs and leaves stuck to their hair and tunics as they rolled around, desperately trying to inflict pain on each other.

What neither boy heard was the dull thud of horses' hooves coming through the forest.

The men on the horses were messengers on an urgent mission for Gwrtheyrn, King of the Island of the Mighty. They pulled up their horses to watch the boys fight, wagering bets on who the champion would be.

"My money's on the blonde lad" said one.

"He won't win," laughed another. "The dark haired boy is a shabby looking wretch but he seems to have more fire in his belly than the bigger lad."

At this point in the fight, Myrddin was actually winning. But then Dinabutius spotted Myrddin's knife lying by the chopped up vine. Myrddin followed his gaze and saw it too. The boys exchanged a look, then both ploughed forwards.

Dinabutius was the quickest. He held the knife in the air and looked at Myrddin.

"Well, boy without a father," he grinned. "What are you going to do now?"

The two messengers nearly fell from their horses when they heard these words. They had travelled for months and months all over the Welsh countryside in search of a fatherless boy. And now in the forests of Carmarthen, could their mission be finally over? But first they had to make sure that they had the right boy.

"Stop fighting, boys!" the messenger ordered, getting down from his horse.

Both boys looked up through the high grass at the powerful horses and were dazzled by the strangers' colourful clothes and the swanky criss-cross of straps on their boots.

"You, boy" he pointed at Myrddin. "Take me to your mother."

Myrddin waited outside the cottage with one of the messengers whilst the other went inside to speak to his mother.

"But the boy must have a father" insisted the messenger. "Are you asking us to believe he has no mortal father?"

"Why do you doubt my words?" she replied.

The messenger sighed and rubbed at his beard.

"Let me get this straight," he said sitting himself down on the wooden stool next to her.

"The night your son was begot, you forgot to cross yourself and the Devil entered your room, and your bed?"

"Yes, My Lord," she said. "Upon Myrddin's life, I have never been with any man in that way - in a way to make me bear a child." Pink coloured her cheeks.

"If I accept what you say as the truth," he rose and looked out through the window at the boy "then he must have inherited his father's powers." He spun around and looked at her. "His evil ways!"

The woman leapt to her feet. Her blue eyes were wide and pleading.

"No, My Lord," she screeched. "Myrddin has inherited certain prophetic powers and the ability to perform magic from his father but he has also inherited my goodness and kindness."

The messenger straightened his cloak and strode to the door. "We are taking the boy with us to Dinas Emrys," he said holding up his hand before she could protest. "King Gwrtheyrn has requested that we bring him a boy without a father. I believe Myrddin to be that boy."

Myrddin's mother could do nothing but watch as the messenger pulled her son onto his horse. A quick kick of heels and the steeds galloped forward. Myrddin's face was the colour of flour as he peered at his mother over his shoulder until she was lost from sight.

The stars twinkled in the sky as Myrddin was helped down from the horse and taken directly to King Gwrtheyrn's make-shift quarters.

"My King," said the messenger, bowing low. "Here is the boy without a father that you seek."

King Gwrtheyrn watched as Myrddin bowed.

"What is your name, boy?" he boomed.

"Myrddin, Sire. Why do you want to see me?"

"Well, my boy, I have a problem that you can help me with. My land has become overrun with Saxon warriors who want me dead."

Myrddin nodded and stared at the magnificent gold torque of office that the King was wearing.

"You're probably wondering what that has to do with you, my boy."

"Yes, Sire," he mumbled. King Gwrtheyrn was a powerful man. Myrddin could not imagine him being frightened of anybody, not even Saxon warriors.

"I am trying to build a tower here to protect myself from the Saxons. My problem is that, however much my stonemasons try and build the tower, the next day when they return there is no sign of their work. The earth simply swallows it up."

Myrddin listened but could not understand what this had to do with him. King Gwrtheyrn could see the boy's confusion and continued with his story.

"My druids have told me to find a fatherless boy" he smiled at Myrddin. "You, my boy."

"I don't understand, Sire."

"Oh, but you will, you will. Let me explain further." King Gwrtheyrn seemed to be struggling to find the right words. "I need your... Well, I need your blood to sprinkle over the stones and mix with the mortar so that my tower won't vanish again."

Myrddin began to feel sick and his head started to pound. He always felt this way when he was about to see into the future.

"Sire, my blood will not secure your tower! Your druids are fools. Bring them to me and I will prove that they are liars."

The druids were summoned and stood in a row before the King.

"Tell me why you think my blood will help to secure the tower" challenged Myrddyn looking from one terrified face to the other. "You," he pointed at the oldest druid "tell me what is obstructing the foundations of the tower."

The druid glanced at King Gwrtheyrn's wide eyes and red face.

"I know not," he whispered, lowering his head.

"I'm no ordinary boy, Sire," Myrddin said to his King. "I can see into the future and I have seen what is making your tower vanish overnight."

King Gwrtheyrn looked deep into Myrddin's eyes, deciding if he could trust the boy.

Myrddin took a deep breath and began his prophecy.

"Sire, underneath the foundations where you are trying to build your tower there is a pool and under the water you will find two hollow stones. In the daytime two dragons sleep, one inside each stone but at night they wake and fight each other. It is because of them that your tower collapses."

King Gwrtheyrn clicked his fingers to a messenger.

"Yes, my King?" he asked.

"I want every available man to dig and find this pool immediately," he ordered.

Several hours later the messenger returned to say the pool had been found. King Gwrtheyrn looked at Myrddin and started to suspect that the boy did have supernatural powers.

"Drain it!" he said "and I will come outside in a short while." The messenger bowed and hurried out of the room. "Well, my boy, your knowledge may well save your life. Let us see if you're right about the dragons."

Myrddin followed King Gwrtheyrn to where his men were working. The pool had been drained and, as Myrddin had prophesied, two stones lay at opposite ends of the hole.

As they watched a red dragon slowly emerged from one stone and a white dragon from the other. They circled the hole, stretching their long necks in their opponent's direction. Enormous bursts of fierce flames rushed from the mouth of the red dragon. The white dragon roared and pawed at the ground with his huge claws then sprang on to the red one's back.

Myrddin clamped his hands over his ears and watched the dragons tearing huge chunks out of each other.

King Gwrtheyrn pulled Myrddin's hands from his ears.

"What is the meaning of the dragons, my boy?" he shouted over the noise.

"The dragons represent the battles between the Britons and Saxons, Sire," Myrddin explained. "Look, the white dragon is the strongest. He represents the Saxons and, for a time, they will have the upper hand. But the red dragon represents the Britons who will overcome them under the leadership of a great King named Arthur."

"Will I meet this King Arthur, my boy?" asked King Gwrtheyrn.

"No, Sire, you will not. Your enemies are close. They will set fire to your tower and you will not escape."

King Gwrtheyrn jumped back at this new prophecy then nodded.

"Go home to your mother now, my boy, and take my blessing with you."

King Gwrtheyrn watched Myrddin walk away. He knew that one day this boy would become a great man and his prophecies would help to keep the Island of the Mighty safe.

RHITTA OF THE BEARDS

Arthur sat up straight in his saddle and looked down the hill at his kingdom. The sight of his court and castle at Caerleon never ceased to fill him with pride. The stone walls looked menacing and he knew any Saxon would think twice about attacking.

He looked to his left at the rapidly flowing water of the River Usk, and could almost feel the cool water lapping on his skin. He loved diving in from the grassy bank and racing across to the other side with his friends, or slithering underwater to the riverbed pretending to be an eel. Things were different now. He had responsibilities and not much time for childish behaviour.

Two years ago, at fifteen, he had been crowned King.

Deep in thought, he pulled at the short curly strands of fair hair on his chin and wished that his beard would grow more quickly. He wanted a long, bushy and important beard like his father once had.

"Have two years really passed since father died?" he asked himself.

Suddenly King Arthur could hear horses charging towards him on the path behind. He twisted around and prepared to reprimand his knights for being so slow.

"My Lord," shouted the first knight to appear, his horse trampling down the wild bluebells that lined the path.

"Prepare yourself for we have visitors!" He pulled on his horse's reins and positioned himself to the right of his King whilst the other knight pressed close on Arthur's left side.

There was no time to ask who was coming. On the path in front of them appeared a messenger accompanied by a troop of armed men. Arthur's fingers slid towards his trusted sword, Excalibur, which hung from his belt.

The troop all wore tunics and cloaks. They each carried a long, shiny sword, and their shields were decorated in the coat of arms of their King.

A messenger who wore the same clothes but had no weapons scrambled down from his horse and stood in front of Arthur.

"My Lord," he bowed low. "I have been s-s-sent with an urgent message from my m-m-master, King Rhitta."

Arthur snorted loudly. He had received a letter from his cousin warning him that trouble was brewing in the north. King Rhitta was not only a tyrant but a giant! He had defeated twenty-eight Kings in battle and was so brutal that he had scraped the beards from their faces and stitched them onto his cloak as a souvenir.

"Well," asked Arthur, trying to keep his voice steady. "What does he want?"

"My Lord, he w-w-wants your beard so that he can finish his c-c-cloak."

"My beard!" Arthur laughed. His father had trained him never to show fear in front of enemies. His hand went to the short curly strands of fair hair on his chin. "My beard is barely grown."

"He w-w-wants your b-b-beard" the messenger repeated, stuttering with nerves.

"Well, he cannot have it" roared Arthur.

Rhitta's soldiers moved forward but the messenger held up his hand for them to stop.

"My Lord," the messenger's complexion had turned a deathly white.
"As you do not agree to give me your b-b-beard then I must warn you that King R-R-Rhitta intends to invade your land and s-s-slay your people unless you agree to fight him in the field at the foot of Aran Benllyn, the day after t-t-tomorrow."

"I will be there. Tell Rhitta that I will die before he has my beard!"

With that Rhitta's men turned their steeds and galloped off, crunching the remainder of the bluebells into the path.

Before long, Arthur's spies reported that Rhitta was marching south with a great army.

"Gather the knights in the Great Hall immediately," barked Arthur. "Go to the kitchens and tell the cooks to bring food and a flagon of mead and tell them to prepare plenty of both to take with us on our journey." Arthur knew the magical powers of the mead and that once his men had drunk it they would each fight as fiercely as nine men.

The noise from the Great Hall greeted Arthur before he entered, wearing his full armour. His men were shouting and spurring on a pretend battle between two of his knights.

Their swords clink clank clinked down the length of the room. They leapt on top of tables, toppling over the remains of the feast onto the floor.

"Enough foolishness," shouted Arthur. "It's time to leave."

The knights assembled themselves into several columns waving their weapons. The flashes from their swords and the sparks from their spears lit the entire night sky. Not one Briton in the Island of the Mighty would fail to see these flashes of lightning - including Rhitta.

"You wanted trouble, Rhitta," Arthur shouted, "now you're going to get it!" Still cheering and shouting they headed north to meet Rhitta's army.

They jabbed at their horses' flanks with their heels. The sudden speed made the horses legs blur. They looked as though they were flying through the air instead of galloping on the ground.

Boom, bang, thud, boom, bang, thud! The noise from their hooves pounding into the grass sounded louder than thunder.

As they neared Aran Benllyn, Arthur's men started as the tree-tops slowly spread apart and they pulled up their horses as a giant head began to show, followed by huge shoulders and body.

It was Rhitta, looking to see what was causing the terrible noise.

"Arthur," he boomed "are you going to give me your beard, or am I to rip it from your face along with your chin?" He advanced forward up-rooting the trees and throwing them to the side as if they were flowers.

"Hurry!" he shouted to his men. "Get your weapons and follow me!" Rhitta's army poked their faces from behind the trees and slowly emerged onto the field.

"What is that sweet smell, Master?" said one. Rhitta sniffed the air and shut his eyes.

"Mead," he said. Rhitta's men knew the power of King Arthur's magical mead and took a step back towards the trees.

Arthur was amazed at the size of his enemy. Rhitta was possibly the biggest and ugliest giant he had ever seen, let alone fought. His red-brown hair was wild and knotted, his eyebrows were like two dirty dead rats and the beard on his face must have been the thickest and bushiest in the whole of the north.

In his hand he held a huge axe. Arthur could see splodges of somebody's blood smeared into the dull silver of the blade. His hand went to the short curly strands of fair hair on his chin as he examined all the beards sewn on to Rhitta's cloak. At the bottom he could see a space for one more beard.

"Rhitta," he said. "My beard is young and not nearly big enough to cover that patch on your cloak." He paused "But I know a beard that is."

"And whose might that be?" he growled.

"Why, your own, of course!" replied Arthur calmly. "What are you going to do – yield or fight?"

"Fight!" Rhitta thundered. "I'm not afraid of you!"

"You should be afraid, Rhitta. You should be very afraid!"

Arthur raised his hand and beckoned his army forward. The almighty thud, thud, thudding of their tread caused the ground to tremble.

Rhitta watched as his army began to shake with fear. One by one they toppled into the brambles on the ground.

"Get up, get up!" he commanded, but they ignored him and tried to hold onto the bucking ground. Some were already crawling back into the safety of the trees.

"I will ask you again, Rhitta," said Arthur. "Do you wish to fight or yield?"

Rhitta looked at the remains of his army and realised they were too afraid to fight. He bowed his head.

"I have no choice but to yield."

King Arthur beckoned, and from the crowd stepped forward Cadwr of Pictland holding a sharp blade.

"Scrape this tyrant's beard from his face and sew it onto his cloak" he ordered.

Blood dripped from Rhitta's chin as he stood disgraced and bare-faced before Arthur.

Both the armies listened as Arthur addressed the giant. "You thought yourself unstoppable because of your size, Rhitta," said Arthur. "The North has been ruled shamefully under your command. Now, as you stand feeling the same humiliation as your conquests, I have one final question."

"Ask your question."

"Rhitta of the beards, tell me who is your Lord and King?"

"You are, My Lord," he bowed low. "Long live King Arthur!"

"Long live King Arthur!" cheered all of the men together.

Rhitta's defeat soon spread through every town and village of the Island of the Mighty. He wore his bearded cloak everywhere he went to show his loyalty to King Arthur. So well-known did Rhitta's shameful story become amongst his countrymen that a proverb was invented about him. The next time that it is snowing and somebody asks how deep is the snow, say that it is 'as thick as Rhitta's beard' and when they ask who Rhitta is, this is the story to tell them.

The story of Brân the Blessed

Arthur took his place at the head of the banquet table and indicated for everybody to sit down. "An awful business today, Sire," said one of Arthur's advisors. "Still it had to be done. We cannot allow those Saxons to come across the North Sea and think that they can do as they please."

"Exactly!" said Arthur snatching a sticky portion of goose from a serving tray. He munched his way through the meat and crunched on the bones. "Word will travel fast of my bravery and the strength of my army. My people need to believe in me, for they have nobody else."

"Well, My Lord, that's not exactly true," said another of the advisors in a loud voice. The music stopped in mid chord, conversations ceased and an icy chill crept across the advisor's shoulders. He glanced sideways at his King and cowered as the goose bone that Arthur had been gnawing was hurled across the table and bounced off his head.

"Tell me what you mean by that!" said Arthur raising himself to his full height. "I am King; nobody else!"

"My Lord, I meant no offence. I was thinking.... I was thinking about Brân the Blessed and the protection of his magic."

"Tell me of Brân the Blessed," said Arthur; "Who is this person?"

"He was King of the Island of the Mighty many years before you were born," continued the advisor, sinking into his seat, "and when he died... when he died, he still wanted to protect his people so he cast a spell, and some say that his magical powers still protect the country today."

"Where is this Brân buried? I will not rest until I have dug him up!"

"Ah, well, it's only his head that has been buried. It's in a casket buried under the White Mount but... but I must warn you that whoever discloses the head of Brân will have nothing but bad luck from that day forward."

"Well that's a risk I am prepared to take" said Arthur. "Go and tell the groom to saddle the horses, and assemble a guard of knights."

"Yes, Sire, but, but… it's raining."

"For heaven sakes, man, do as I order." The blue veins in Arthur's temple thumped.

The dogs barked excitedly and criss-crossed around the horses' feet as the rain lashed and fought Arthur and his men every step of the way towards the White Mount in London.

Arthur sneezed and shivered as he stood in front of the White Mount. He had never been so soaked in his life. The rain water on his clothes made it difficult for him to move his limbs.

At least the wetness of the earth would make it easier to dig up the head.

He could ask one of his knights to do the digging but he did not want to. It was important that he disclosed the head himself.

"I have to do it!" he roared; "I have to. Don't you see that my people need to believe in me and me alone?"

He began to scrape away the soil with a shovel and then with his bare hands.

The intensity of the storm increased. Rain slashed at his back and thunder deafened his ears but Arthur kept digging. His hands were thick with mud and the smell of the wet grass was making him feel sick but he could not stop.

He dug and scraped and dug and scraped until his bleeding fingers finally rapped on the wooden lid of a casket.

At last," he cried.

Arthur rolled the casket over to examine it. The hinges had turned a dull brown but the wood was still solid underneath his fingers despite its age.

Lightning illuminated the casket as Arthur forced the creaking lid open. Twisting his fingers into the gap, Arthur yanked and the lid disintegrated in his hand.

Arthur's hand fell across his mouth as the head of Brân was revealed.

The dogs growled and the knights gasped as they stepped forward for a closer look. Foul, musty air invaded their lungs making them gag.

Brân's eyes were shut and black slugs slithered across his eyes. His filthy orangey-coloured hair and beard were knotted with worms.

The head was huge!

"Get back," ordered Arthur to his men, raising his arm.

Two enormous brown eyes sprang open and met his own.

"You!" whispered Brân.

Arthur leapt backwards as Brân's ginger eyelashes, thicker than whips, lashed as he blinked sleep, and slugs, from his eyes.

"How dare you challenge my authority? How dare you disclose my head?"

"I dare do anything for I am Arthur, King of the Island of the Mighty."

"You will pay a great penalty for your recklessness, boy."

Arthur looked at the head of the old ruler and shuddered. His whispery voice was slow and croaky but Arthur could hear every word despite the noise from the storm.

"You have disclosed my head. You must now listen to my story," he said.

"Nobody tells me what to do. Your story is of no interest to me."

"You insolent boy. My power will no longer protect...."

"I don't want your help! I alone protect my people" Arthur said, scratching the dirt from his own hair.

"But be warned, my boy! To protect... to protect..." The huge giant seemed to become lost in his memories. "I did everything to protect my sister" he whispered. "How that girl suffered."

"I have told you that I do not wish to hear your story."

"What harm can listening to his story do, My Lord?" said one of his men. "We have travelled far; his tale may cheer our mood."

Arthur sighed and looked at Bran's staring eyes.

"Tell us your tale, old King" he said.

Arthur pulled his cloak tightly around his chin and sneezed. He and his knights sat huddled in front of the old ruler. Nature was still beating them relentlessly.

Brân cleared his throat and sighed. His long ginger eyelashes mingled in with his burnt-orange beard.

"Branwen, my sister, was such a lovely girl. Her friends filled my court at Harlech daily. Their laughter rattled through the hedgerows. They pranced and danced and sang. Like a bird, Branwen sang. Her hair shone the same colour as the stars. Her eyes were a deeper blue than the sea. She was known throughout the land for her beauty and across the sea they spoke of her too. One day a rainbow appeared in the water. So beautiful were its colours: red, blue, yellow and, and... I forget. But then I realised it could not be a rainbow for the sun shone - and no rain had fallen. Straining my eyes I made out distant sails. It was a fleet of ships sailing in from the west. They carried King Matholwch of Ireland, the Island of the Fair. He had heard of Branwen's beauty and he wanted her for his bride. Of course, such an alliance would benefit the Island of the Mighty."

"We do not need help. We protect our own," said Arthur.

"Needing assistance should not cause shame, boy."

"It shows a weakness that a King should never show."

"You have much to learn."

"Get on with the story, Brân."

"Matholwch and Branwen married and there was much rejoicing, but trouble started the next morning. Efnysien, our half-brother, returned from a journey from, from… I forget where. He was like a madman. "She should not have been married without my consent" he kept saying. He had his revenge. Oh yes, he had his revenge. He went to the stables and found Matholwch's horses. He used a knife. Poor creatures, it pained the eye to see them."

"The beggar," said Arthur. "Matholwch must have been very angry at this insult."

"Indeed he was. The insult was felt as deeply by me. What I feared for the most was Branwen's safety. Matholwch must not be allowed to leave still angry. He may take his revenge out on her. So, I replaced his horses and I made him a gift of silver. He was still unhappy and said few words. The thought of Branwen being mistreated was too much so I offered him my cauldron."

"Your cauldron?" asked Arthur, amazed.

"This was no ordinary cauldron. It had magical powers. Power to bring dead men back to life! If you died today and were thrown into the cauldron, tomorrow you would be recovered. You would be struck dumb but that is a small price to pay."

"Where is this cauldron of rebirth now?" asked Arthur thinking that he would very much like to be the owner of such a special treasure.

"Matholwch took it over the sea."

"Branwen must have been worshipped by Matholwch after you gave him such a wonderful gift," said Arthur.

Brân's eyes reddened and he tried to blink away tears. It obviously pained him to think about his sister.

"Branwen sat on board Matholwch's ship on a golden throne as she waved me good-bye. It may have been red…I forget. I prayed that she would find happiness with her new husband. I prayed even harder that he would love and treat her well. Within a year a boy was born and they called him Gwern.

But then Matholwch's foster brothers threatened a rebellion. They insisted that Matholwch took revenge for the maiming of his horses. And he did take revenge on poor Branwen. She was treated no better than a slave. Matholwch hit her once. The butcher beat her daily."

"How did you learn about this ill-treatment?"

"I was in my chambers one morning when a starling flew in through the open window. 'Brân, Brân, Brân!' it screeched then landed on my shoulder. It may have been my head…I forget. Branwen had reared the bird. She taught it how to speak and recognise me. Did I tell you that she sang like a bird? I loved to hear her sing.

I prepared an army and we sailed west towards the Island of the Fair. No ship was big enough to hold me. I simply had to wade across the water.

Matholwch's men appeared on the coast with greetings. There was a dark and eerie sense of foreboding. My only concern was rescuing Branwen. How that poor girl had suffered. What happened next is beyond comprehension."

A shudder ran down Arthur's back. He knew that there was going to be no happy-ever-after.

"Finish your story, Brân," he said.

"Matholwch had to compensate me for his mistreatment of Branwen. He built me a house. I have never before been able to fit inside any house. A huge fire crackled. It was welcoming. His kingdom he gave to Gwern. He was a fine looking chap. The boy came forwards and kissed my cheek. He did not go to Efnysien. It was I who told the child to greet his uncle."

The hairs on Arthur's neck rose.

"Gwern tiptoed across to his uncle. Efnysien picked him up and without warning threw him head first into the flames of the fire where he died."

Arthur gasped and for a moment he could find no words.

"Tell me before I go," he said. "What happened to you and Branwen?"

"Branwen, oh, Branwen," he said. Tears rolled from his red eyes. "She died in the ship travelling home of a broken heart. In the battle that followed the slaying of Gwern a poisoned spear had clipped my right foot. There was no hope for me, I knew that. I ordered my men to cut off my head and bring it here to bury it on the White Mount with my eyes facing across the sea. It is by this magic that I am able to protect the Island of Mighty."

"But I'm here to protect this land now. I and my army protect the people."

"You have disclosed my head, Arthur. It is too late for you. Bad luck and misfortune will be your constant companions."

Brân's face sank as he closed his eyes and not another word did he say.

The Battle of Camlan

King Arthur sprang from his chair and dragged the messenger to the floor. He yanked the dagger from his belt and pressed the tip of the shiny blade to the boy's throat.

"Repeat what you have stated," he said.

The messenger, a sandy haired youth of no more than fourteen years, gaped at Arthur through bulging eyes and shook his head.

"Please, My Lord," begged the lad "do not kill me for I am only the bearer of news!"

Arthur's teeth ground together as he tried to control his temper. He removed the dagger from the boy's throat so that he could repeat his words.

"Speak!"

"My Lord, Mawdred has claimed your throne for himself. He has sent word overseas to send many warriors with the promise of land and treasure in return for their help. My King, eight hundred ships armed with thousands of soldiers have already landed on the Island of the Mighty. They are there now awaiting your return!"

Arthur released the grip that he had on the messenger's tunic and staggered to his feet. His feet felt like they were cast in clay as he stumbled towards the open window. He sighed as the cool breeze caressed his hair. "Betrayed by my own nephew" he thought.

"Get out of here," said Arthur. He glanced over his shoulder and watched the messenger trip over his feet as he walked backwards, bowing, towards the arched doorway.

"Thank you, My Lord." A trickle of blood slithered from his throat and clashed with the green tunic that he was trying to rearrange on his skinny body.

Arthur turned back towards the window and placed his palms either side of the opening. He was not aware that his knight, Sir Bedwyr, had approached until he felt a hand on his shoulder.

"Come, Sire," said Bedwyr. "we will easily slaughter these beggars before breakfast has begun." Arthur shrugged off Bedwyr's hand.

"How can Mawdred do this to me?" said Arthur, not looking at his knight. "I trusted him with my kingdom and he repays me like this!"

"He was always jealous of your power, My Lord," said Bedwyr.

Arthur slammed his fists into the stone wall. "I will kill Mawdred for this." He clicked his fingers to an advisor. "Assemble the men for we return to the Island of the Mighty immediately."

The Great Battle of Camlan began as Arthur and his army turned the curved bend by the lake.

"Get into your divisions," said Arthur. Into the mouth of madness they marched and charged. The cavalry soldiers attacked as infantry men fell. Riderless horses reared onto hind hooves and trampled over hundreds of fallen bodies as they fled.

Through the dust and mayhem, Arthur's muscles rippled as he fought. Two, three, sometimes four soldiers attacked as one. No sword could match Excalibur's speed and scores of the men died trying.

"We have them beaten," yelled Arthur, turning in the direction of Bedwyr as the warriors started to retreat.

"Look out, My Lord," shouted Bedwyr, yanking his sword from a ginger haired soldier's side as Mawdred's axe plunged into the ground besides Arthur. Mawdred stood a few feet away, his sword and shield positioned for battle.

"You beggar, Mawdred," said Arthur, turning to meet him. "Why have you done this?" Excalibur too was now poised and ready.

"You may have brought peace to the Island of the Mighty, Arthur," said Mawdred; "but it is a peace won by war, which rarely lasts. You have made many enemies — and I am one." He loosened the cord at his neck and shrugged a green cloak from his shoulders.

The two men circled each other warily.

"You think that you are man enough to beat me, Mawdred?"

"I know that I am!" Mawdred's sword smashed against Excalibur with such force that Arthur staggered back a step. "I will be King of the Britons."

Arthur steadied himself and a fierce fight began. The blades of both swords flashed. Mawdred ducked and Arthur twisted. Sparks flew from the blades as they clashed. Mawdred kneed Arthur in the stomach. Arthur rammed Mawdred's head into a tree. They gripped each other's legs and wrestled on the ground. Neither would yield. Then Excalibur's blade struck Mawdred a fatal wound that his shied could not protect. With his last breath Mawdred mustered all his strength and brought the pommel of his sword down onto Arthur's head with a sickening crunch.

The two warlords crumpled together and lay side by side on the ground. The battle still raged but Mawdred could no longer hear the sound of swords and spears and axes inflicting their pain.

"My Lord," said Bedwyr, rushing to the side of his King. "Arthur, can you hear me?" He ran a hand down his face and saw the blood gushing from Arthur's head. Pulling off his own cloak he pressed the thick material onto the gash.

Arthur's eyes flickered and he could see two Bedwyr's peering over him. "The noises are growing fainter and fainter. The battle must be over" he thought through the pain. Bedwyr could see Arthur's lips moving.

"Come, My Lord, save your strength" he said. "There will be plenty of time for talking later."

Bedwyr grunted as he heaved Arthur from the ground and threw him over his shoulder. He staggered through the dying and the dead, moving away from the fighting.

"Enough," said Arthur, "lay me down."

Bedwyr gently placed his master at the foot of a tree, not far from the lake.

He pressed his cloak back onto his master's wound.

"Bedwyr," said Arthur. Bedwyr put his ear close to Arthur's mouth. "Take my sword, Excalibur. Throw it into the lake and return to tell me what you have seen."

"Yes, My King." Bedwyr dashed towards the edge of the lake. He raised his arm and stopped. Glancing around, Bedwyr lowered Excalibur and examined the craftsmanship. "No good will come of throwing such a magnificent sword into the water" he thought. He looked for a hiding place and spotted a clump of brambles. He pushed the sword inside, scratching his arm, and returned to his King.

"I have done the deed, My Lord," he said.

"What did you see?"

"Nothing, Sire," said Bedwyr. "The water swallowed the sword."

Arthur opened his eyes and looked at his knight.

"Bedwyr, go back to the lake. Throw in the sword. Excalibur cannot fall into corrupt hands. Please, do this one last thing for me."

"Yes, My Lord." Bedwyr pulled the sword from the brambles but could not bear the thought of such a rich and noble sword going under the water. "My King is mortally wounded" he thought. "He will never know."

Arthur's breathing was becoming shallower but he opened his eyes as Bedwyr approached.

"Tell me what you saw."

"My Lord, I heard a splash and saw the swallows take flight."

Again, Arthur knew that Bedwyr was lying and ordered him back to the lake.

"Bedwyr, I am your King. I command you. Throw the sword into the lake."

At the water's edge Bedwyr ran his fingers over the hilt of Excalibur. "This sword is not mine to keep" he thought as he threw the sword with all his might and watched as Excalibur swished and turned in the air.

He gasped as swirling ripples formed and a white slender arm rose from the lake.

The hand grasped Excalibur's hilt and in slow motion descended into the water. Bedwyr raced back to Arthur's side. He pulled Arthur against his lap and told his master what he had witnessed.

"Thank you, Bedwyr. Thank you. The Lady of Lake will care for Excalibur." Bedwyr wiped the blood from Arthur's lips as he started to cough. "My friend, take me to the edge of the lake."

As Bedwyr, with Arthur over his shoulder, approached the lake a barge floated to the water's edge with three fair maids on board. One of them was Gwenhwyfar, the love of Arthur's life.

"Lay me in the barge," said Arthur, near to death. "Take comfort. My wounds may heal. The Island of Avalon has magical powers. But, if you never hear from me again, pray, my loyal friend, for my eternal soul."

"Do not speak that way, your wounds will heal," said Bedwyr. He gripped Arthur's hand.

"We must leave now," said Gwenhwyfar. She covered Arthur with a blanket and began to stroke his hair. "Please push us afloat, Sir Bedwyr."

"No, no, not yet," he said, staring at his King. "Please...."

"Sir Bedwyr, be strong. Arthur needs you now more than ever."

Reluctantly, Bedwyr climbed out and gave a gentle push. He watched as the barge started to drift away into the falling mist.

"No...., oh no, please God." He plunged into the water and started to swim but the harder he swam the further away the barge drifted. There was no choice but to turn back.

Bedwyr slumped onto the bank of the lake. He strained his eyes but the barge was no longer in sight. "Who will protect the Island of the Mighty now that King Arthur has gone?" he wailed silently. His head sagged and his huge shoulders started to shudder. He could not help but grieve for his king and what might become of his kingdom.

A slow, deep beating of a drum broke the silence of the lake. The battle still raged and was coming closer.

"Until Arthur returns" he said, "I will protect the Island of the Mighty." Leaping to his feet, he picked up his sword and strode through the trees, back into the thick of the fighting.

TALIESIN AND THE FLOODING OF CANTRE GWAELOD

The feast in the Great Hall was in full flow as the rain lashed against the shutters. Seithennin, the King's watchman, was enjoying himself. He sang along to the music, laughed at the court jester, and pulled a serving wench wearing a blood-red dress onto his knee. She giggled at his jokes and refilled the goblet that he held out.

This was Seithennin's eighth drink and he was very drunk.

"The storm is worsening," said a soldier, rushing into the hall; shaking rainwater from his hair. He saw Seithennin sitting at a bench in the far corner with the wench bouncing on his knee.

"Seithennin," he said. "Have you seen the storm? Is the dyke safe?"

Every year the sea crept closer and threatened to drown the town. It was Seithennin's job to open and close the sluice gates of the dyke that protected King Gwyddno Garanhir's fertile land at Cantre'r Gwaelod from being flooded. A special watchtower, with a huge bell, had been built so that if a hole did appear in the dyke, the bell would alert the villagers who would come running and fill the hole.

"Go away, man," said Seithennin. "Can you not see that I am busy?"

Seithennin's eyes were blood-shot and his speech was slurred.

"But…."

"Leave me alone," he shouted and accidentally knocked over his goblet with the back of his hand. The soldier watched as Seithennin placed his lips onto the table and sucked the spilt wine into his mouth.

"But have you shut the sluice gates?" said the soldier. The sluice gates were opened every day at low tide to allow water to be drained from the land. But they must be closed again as the tide returned or the sea would gush into the village.

"Oh, my word," said Seithennin, clamping a hand to his mouth. "Oh no, I have forgotten." He sprang to his feet so suddenly that the poor wench toppled backwards from his lap and lay sprawled across the floor.

Seithennin did not even glance at her but raced through the crowds towards the door, followed by the soldier. They found the stable boy cowering in a doorway with a straw sack from the stables covering his head. The lad's face was raw from the heavy beating he had endured from the stinging rain.

"Fetch our horses," shouted Seithennin. He repeated the request three times before the boy heard over the noise of the storm.

The wind and rain was so fierce that Seithennin and the soldier were nearly blown from their saddles a number of times as they raced towards the dyke.

They rode like men possessed under the blackest sky that had ever been seen. Not one star shone to guide their way. As they galloped along, shouting at their flagging horses, Seithennin cursed himself for being so foolish with the drink, and vowed that he would not touch another drop of wine as long as he lived.

"Seithennin, Seithennin," shouted the soldier. "I think that I can hear the rushing of the sea."

"Go back," bawled Seithennin, "warn King Gwyddno that the dyke may have burst. I have to go and see." The soldier spun his horse around as Seithennin disappeared into the darkness.

It was not until the soldier had reached high ground that he stopped. A bolt of lightning flashed across the sky and, in the distance, he could see an enormous wall of black waves. He knew that Seithennin could not survive the ferocity of those waves and, in truth, he had little sympathy for the watchman who had neglected his duties to drink wine. Without a second glance, he raced to tell his King that Cantre'r Gwaelod was being flooded by the sea.

With the help of the soldier, King Gwyddno and his son, Elfin, escaped to higher ground. But sadly, many of the villagers and soldiers drowned along with their villages.

Life for the King changed forever that night and he led a much poorer life. He no longer had his fertile fields to supply the villagers with food. Instead, they depended on salmon, cod and herring from the River Dyfi.

One day Elfin, the King's son, was sitting on the river bank fishing. He squinted at the sun and listened to the soft ripple of the water. He had not caught any fish and decided to walk further along the bank to try his luck there. As he cast in his line he heard a baby crying, and looked around to see who was approaching.

"That's strange," he said. He cocked his head to the side and listened carefully. "There it is again."

Feeling a tug on his fishing rod, he glanced down into the water.

Elfin rubbed his eyes in disbelief. "What on earth...."

For there, tangled in his line, was a little leather bag and the crying, Elfin was convinced, was coming from inside.

He lay on his stomach and pulled the line closer until he could grasp the bag. Elfin kneeled over the bag and carefully opened the drawstring. The first thing that he saw was a forehead, a radiant forehead.

"What a radiant forehead you have," said Elfin, running his finger across it.

"Well," said a tiny voice. "Tâl means forehead and iesin means radiant or fine. There, let my name be Taliesin."

Elfin did not answer but stared open mouthed at the baby. Never in his life had he met a baby that could talk.

"Taliesin, Taliesin," he sang. "I like that name, for it is far nicer than my old name."

Elfin's expression had not changed. It was as if he had been turned to stone. A talking baby was hard to comprehend never mind a singing one.

"Old name?" he finally managed to ask. "Who are you?"

"My old name was Gwion and I was an ordinary type of boy before the witch, Ceridwen, took me from my village and made me look after her cauldron. She was making a magic potion that had to bubble away for one year and a day."

Elfin took the baby from the bag and sat him on his knee.

"You're a boy born from magic," he said. There was nothing unusual about witchcraft and wizardry in those old dark days. "But how did you come to be in the river"?

"Ceridwen's son, Morfan, was ugly and rude and stupid. Ceridwen had no spell that would make him handsome or sociable and she worried that he would not be accepted into King Arthur's court. She found an old spell in her great, great grandmother's book of magic that would turn him into the most intelligent man in the world. I am very thirsty. Do you have a drink, Elfin?"

"Not here, no," he said, wondering how this startling baby knew his name. "But you can come and live in my father's castle with us."

Elfin put the baby back into the bag, placed the fishing rod over his shoulder and walked slowly along the river bank, listening as Taliesin continued with his tale.

"Ceridwen's cauldron simmered away for a year and a day but only the first three drops of the potion could be used for the magic to work. The day that the spell was ready, Morfan was being his rude, obnoxious self. So I shoved him to the stone floor. As he was climbing to his feet, the cauldron gave out an ear piercing scream and the three magic drops leapt from the cauldron and landed on my little finger. They were so hot that I put my finger into my mouth and, and well, swallowed the magic drops that were meant to make Morfan intelligent."

"I bet Ceridwen was furious with you," said Elfin.

"Luckily, she was not in the room," said Taliesin, and gave a slight chuckle. "My head was about to explode with all the new knowledge that I had acquired. I knew everything about everything. I also knew one thing for sure. I had to leave before Ceridwen discovered what had happened."

"Goodness me," said Elfin. "She would have killed you if she had the chance."

"She nearly did. I ran from her cottage as fast as my legs would carry me. I thought that I had escaped but then her screeching came from behind: "Gwion, you little toad. Wait till I get my hands on you." I turned, and there she was, hurtling towards me. There was no way that I could outrun her and wished that I was a hare. No sooner had the thought entered my head that I was transformed into a hare. Gone were my legs and hands, I now had paws, with claws, and two big furry ears replaced my own."

"Did you lose her?"

"No. Ceridwen is a very talented witch and transformed herself into a greyhound. I swear, Elfin, I hopped as fast as I could but Ceridwen's snarling teeth were a millimetre away from my tail."

"Oh, my word," said Elfin. "How did you escape?"

"The river was in front of me so I leapt off the bank and willed myself to be a fish. By the time I hit the water, my ears and tail were replaced by fins. I cut through the water as fast as fast I could and then I heard a splash. Ceridwen was no longer a greyhound but an otter. I darted through the river in every direction possible to lose her but I could not. She was a centimetre away. I wished myself a bird and shot through the water into the air. Ceridwen had bigger plans. She transformed into a brown hawk with flapping wings that were much stronger than mine."

Elfin stopped and put the rod and Taliesin's bag onto the floor. He pulled the boy from the bag and cradled him close to his heart.

"I know. It gets worse too. Ceridwen chased me through the sky until my wings could flap no more. I prayed to God for help as Ceridwen whooshed and twirled all around me. There was nowhere to hide, no strength left to fly."

Taliesin's voice crackled as he relived his adventure. "Then, when I had given up hope, I saw a farmyard below with a pile of corn seed by a shed. I stopped flapping my wings and fell from the sky, praying to be turned into a tiny piece of corn seed as I landed on the ground. Gone were my feathers and I hit the pile of corn seed quite heavily, sinking to the bottom of the pile. Ceridwen crashed from the sky seconds later and landed on top of the pile. I was no longer at the bottom but scattered across the farmyard with the other grains of seed. The next words that I heard filled my heart with dread."

"Change these feathers to that of a red-brown hen," said Ceridwen, in her creepy voice.

"She started to scratch at the ground, swallowing every grain of seed in sight, including me," said Taliesin. "For nine months I lay in Ceridwen's stomach, shaking as I listened to what she intended to do to me once I was born. She had transformed back into a witch and planned a slow lingering act of revenge for the three magical drops that should have been Morfan's."

"Well," said Elfin. "You are still alive. Tell me, for I am intrigued, how did you manage to survive Ceridwen's clutches?"

"When I was born the first thing that I saw was Ceridwen's face scowling down at me, so I smiled and gurgled like I was glad to see her. I had to be clever and make her love me, so that she would not have the heart to kill me. Morfan would have killed me like a shot but Ceridwen would not let him. In the end, to keep her son happy, she agreed that I should be thrown into the sea and left to fend for myself."

"Thank goodness that I heard your cry," said Elfin, "or you may have ended your days as fish food." He put Taliesin back into the bag and carried on walking back to his father's castle.

"Do not be disappointed that you caught no fish today, Elfin, for I am a far greater catch than any fish."

As Taliesin grew older the fortunes of King Gwyddno's tribe prospered. The boy became an important member of the King's household. He grew to be a bard, a poet, a singer of songs, and a great storyteller. In part, it is because of his stories and poetry that the legend of King Arthur lives on today.

THE CAVE WHERE KING ARTHUR SLEEPS

Many, many years after King Arthur ruled the Island of the Mighty, a young man, whose real name cannot be disclosed for legal reasons, became excited by a conversation that he overheard between two travellers who stopped at his hovel.

The young man, whom we will call Dewi, wanted to have plenty of money but did not want to work to gain any. His small cottage was shabby and dirty, very much like his appearance. The land that surrounded his cottage was overgrown with clumps of dried weeds, and a few half-starved chickens wandered around unhappily. They clucked and pecked at the ground in the hope of finding a grain of seed to eat.

Dewi hid behind the barn door as he watched the strangers dismount and lead their horses to the water trough in the yard which was crumbling with age.

They did not know that Dewi was listening or they would not have spoken so freely.

"They say that there is a cave where King Arthur sleeps, waiting for the day when he is needed to bring justice to a troubled world" said one. "If that is true then where on earth is it? We have searched everywhere and there's nowhere left to look."

"Have patience, my friend," said the other. "We can't give up now. Listen, all we need to do is find the tree whose bark resembles a face. King Arthur, and all his lovely gold and silver are buried nearby."

Dewi's ears pricked up at the mention of gold and silver. He watched as the man pulled a piece of paper from his pocket. "Look," he said, as the other came closer and followed his companion's pointing finger. "The tree with the face is here and six steps to the left, hidden behind an old hazel tree, is the entrance to the cave."

"Yes, I know, you told me. But what's the point of knowing where the entrance is if we can't find the blasted tree. Perhaps it's for the best. They say that King Arthur lies surrounded by hundreds of his knights, if we awoke them, they would be furious." The stranger gave a shudder.

"No, no they would not. Not as long as we remembered to tell them to keep sleeping as it is not yet time."

"We will search over the hill by the stream," said the first man. "And then I am going home for I am fed-up of looking for something that probably does not exist."

Dewi waited until the strangers were out of sight and pulled a three-legged stool into the barn doorway.

"A tree that resembles a face," he said, rubbing his chin. "I believe I know where such a tree grows." He began to chuckle to himself, "and it is nowhere near the stream but in the opposite direction, hidden behind the hills and rocks."

With the thought of having King Arthur's gold and silver bulging in his pocket, Dewi ran from the barn, leapfrogged over the post that held his crumbling fence, and ran across the field in the direction where he hoped to find the tree that resembled a face.

The tree was not hard to find, for Dewi knew the area well and had played there as a boy. He stood in front of the tree and rubbed his chin.

"This has to be the one," he said. "I can clearly make out a face, two bulging knots in the wood for eyes, a branch for a nose, and that smooth circular O sunken into the tree trunk definitely resembles an open mouth."

Dewi's mouth suddenly mirrored the tree.

"Now, did the stranger say that the entrance was six steps to the left, or six steps to the right?"

He counted six steps to the right, and started to tear at the sharp brambles that covered nothing but a rock face.

"It must be six to the left," he said, licking the blood from his fingers as he returned to the tree.

"One, two, three, four, five, six," he counted, and stopped in front of an old hazel tree. "This is it," he screamed. "I remember now, the strangers said that the entrance is behind an old hazel tree."

Dewi squeezed his body behind the hazel tree and pushed at the rock face.

Nothing.

He went back to the tree that resembled a face, and recounted six steps to the left.

"Behind the hazel tree…." he said, looking at the ground. "I wonder?"

Dewi searched through the undergrowth until he found a thick stick. He knelt at the back of the hazel tree and plunged the stick deep into the earth. After digging for a solid hour, a dull light began to shine through the hole. Spurred on by the thought of the gold and silver, Dewi's digging became frantic. He dug and dug until blisters appeared on the palms of his hands.

"Finally," he said, and gazed down onto a flight of stone steps that led deep underground. He climbed slowly down the steps, stopping occasionally and listening. "It sounds like breathing."

At the bottom of the steps, the dull light illuminated his way as he tiptoed along a narrow passageway. Dewi could see a huge bell hanging from the roof and instinct told him not to make it ring as he squeezed past. Towards the end of the passage the light turned from dull to blinding. Shielding his eyes, Dewi stepped into a cave and found the source of the light.

"Oh, my word," he said.

There in the middle of the cave lay King Arthur, deep in sleep, surrounded by his sleeping knights. The light shone from the silver swords and armour that every man had by him, waiting for the day that they would be called when the Britons were in trouble.

Dewi crept into the cave, and stared at the piles of gold and silver.

"Oh! I will be a wealthy man for the rest of my life," he cried, shoving handfuls of gold into his pockets and anywhere else that he could find.

In fact, his pockets bulged so much with the gold that he accidentally knocked the bell with his elbow as he tried to leave the cave.

"Is it time?" said one of King Arthur's knights.

Dewi froze, and his heart started to thump.

"No, sleep on brave knight for it is not yet time," he said.

Dewi held his breath while he listened to the knight settle back down onto the floor. As he crept along the passage and back up the stone steps, he swore that he would never return.

But as soon as the last piece of gold was spent, Dewi found himself at the top of the stone steps, and scuttling along the passageway towards Arthur's treasures. He squeezed past the bell and looked around the cave. Everything was as he had left it. Arthur still lay surrounded by the knights. Nobody had moved a muscle.

"I will take only silver this time," he said, pouncing on a pile of silver coins and goblets that were near the entrance of the cave.

When he could carry no more, he stood and looked at the bell.

"I must be careful not to knock the bell again, for I may not be so lucky this time."

Dewi tried to be careful but his body was made so fat by all the silver that the bell clanged, only louder this time.

"Is it the day? Are the Cymry in danger?" boomed a knight.

Dewi shut his eyes and clenched his teeth.

"No, sleep on brave knight for it is not yet time."

Again, Dewi held his breath while the knight lay back down.

And again, he swore that he would never return to the cave.

But like all foolish people, Dewi squandered the money from the silver, in the same manner as he had done with the gold, on silly luxuries and high living. His cottage was still rundown, the fence had fallen down, and the remaining few of his chickens barely had the strength to peck at the ground, they were so hungry.

"I will go back to the cave one last time," he said, when there was no food left in his cupboard, or more importantly to the waster, not a drop of wine to drink.

For the third time, Dewi climbed down the stone steps and scurried towards the bright light that would make him rich again. He squeezed past the golden bell and looked around. The scene was the same, as though King Arthur and his men were set in stone.

"This time, I will take as much gold and silver as I can carry," he said.

Dewi could hardly walk his pockets were so full. He stopped at the bell and tried to press himself further into the passageway wall.

But it was no use. The greedy young man knocked the bell yet again.

Only this time the bell clanged even louder and for so long that Dewi clamped his hands over his ears.

"King Arthur," said a knight. "Is it time to awake, are the Cymry in danger?"

Dewi did not have time to speak, for there, in the entrance to the cave, stood King Arthur. His huge frame almost blocked the gleam of light from the treasures and Dewi cowered as the passageway suddenly became quite dark. But not dark enough to miss the look of disgust that spread across King Arthur's face.

"No," said King Arthur. "The time is not yet. Come and see the creature that has taken our gold and silver."

King Arthur moved out of the entranceway so that Dewi could see the commotion that he had caused with his wicked ways.

Dewi shook from head to toe as he watched the knights scrambling to their feet.

"Would you march out for him?" asked King Arthur.

"No, Sire, no Sire," shouted the king's men together.

Dewi watched as one by the one the knights and soldiers pulled out their swords.

"Shall we finish him, My Lord," said one.

"No," said King Arthur. "Shake our gold and silver from his person and then throw him out."

Two of the knights picked Dewi up by his ankles and shook him until every last piece of the stolen treasure fell from his clothing. Then, still by the ankles, they carried him up the stone steps, making sure that his head bumped against every one. Outside, the knights lay Dewi on his back and each grabbed an arm and a leg. They swung him to and fro, to build up speed, and then they let go. Dewi hurtled through the air not knowing where he was going. He soon realised what he had landed in. Every one of the stinging nettles stung at his arms, his legs, his face, his backside, you name any part of the body and that's where the nettles attacked.

Nobody but an utter fool would have attempted to enter the cave for a fourth time.

Dewi was an utter fool. His greed for more gold and silver spurred him back to the entrance of the cave. He thought nothing of King Arthur's wrath or how lucky he was to be let off so leniently the last time. He thought only of the money and what he would buy. However, try as he might, Dewi could never find the entrance to the cave where King Arthur sleeps.

The search for the cave continues to this day, but it has never been found.

ORIGINS
OF THE TALES

MYRDDIN AND THE TWO DRAGONS

The story of the two dragons first appeared in the *History of the Britons* and is believed to have been written at the beginning of the ninth century by Nennius, a monk from Bangor, North Wales. Geoffrey of Monmouth, a cleric and teacher, continues with Nennius's two dragon myth in his *History of the Kings of Britain*, which he completed at the beginning of the twelfth century.

As with most myths and legends the details of the stories, names and locations vary depending on the author. Nennius names the fatherless boy as Ambrose, whereas Geoffrey calls him by his more popular name Merlin but adds that the boy "was also called Ambrosius." The Welsh version of the name is Myrddin, and he is known to be the son of a devil and the woman who did not cross herself, though very few details are mentioned about her origins in the Arthurian romances.

RHITTA OF THE BEARDS

The 'giant' Rhitta Fawr is one of King Arthur's biggest rivals. He briefly appeared in *The History of the Kings of Britain* as Retho, and in Thomas Malory's *Le Morte d'Arthur* as 'Kynge Royns of Northe Walis'. A full account of the story is given in Gwen Jones's *Stories from Wales*.

THE STORY OF BRÂN

The story of Bendigeidfran, Brân the Blessed, is told in the *Mabinogion*, an important collection of stories that have evolved over the centuries by different storytellers. Their origins are rumoured to go back to the Iron Age. In this book, Brân is introduced in the story *Branwen Daughter of Llŷr*. He is also mention in the *Triad of Three Fortunate Concealments* (where the severed head is buried to protect Britain from invading armies) and in the *Three Unfortunate Disclosures* (where King Arthur digs up the head) found in early medieval texts.

THE DEATH OF ARTHUR

A detailed account of The Battle of Camlan is recorded in Geoffrey's *The History of the Kings of Britain*. However, in Geoffrey's version, Mawdred is killed and the battle continues. It is slightly later that King Arthur is 'mortally wounded and was carried to the Isle of Avalon'. Some research suggests that Afallon/Avalon is Bardsey Island, off the western tip of the Llŷn Peninsula.

THE BIRTH OF TALIESIN

Taliesin is believed to have been a sixth-century poet, and outside of Welsh tradition was practically ignored until he was rediscovered by modern writers. An excellent, illustrated book written by Gwyn Thomas and Kevin Crossley-Holland, *The Tale of Taliesin* gives a greater insight into Taliesin's escape from Ceridwen, and his life at Gwyddno Garanhir's court.

THE CAVE WHERE KING ARTHUR SLEEPS

The legend of where King Arthur's cave actually is varies, and it has been located in many places. In Welsh legend, the cave is usually situated at Lliwedd in Snowdonia. The tale of the young Welshman who enters the cave is generally the same. He discovers the cave, steals and squanders the gold and silver, and through his greed re-enters and wakes King Arthur from his sleep, with unpleasant consequences. The most detailed account of this story is written by Gwyn Jones in his *Stories from Wales*.

FURTHER READING

Jones, Gwyn, Crossley-Holland, Kevin, *The Tale of Taliesin*
(London: Gollancz Children's Paperbacks: 1992)

Jones, Gwyn, *Stories from Wales*
(Oxford: Oxford University Press, 2009)

Malory, Thomas, *Le Morte d'Arthur*, ed. By Stephen H. A. Shepherd
(USA: Norton, 2004)

Monmouth, Geoffrey of, *The History of the Kings of Britain*, trans. by Lewis
Thorpe, (London: Penguin, 1966)

The Arthurian Encyclopaedia, ed. by Norris, J. Lacy
(New York & London: Garland Pub, Inc, 1986)

The Mabinogion, trans. by Jeffrey Gantz,
(London: Penguin, 1976)

Symonds, Roger, et al. *King Arthur's Labyrinth*,
(Corris Caverns Ltd. 2016)